...S A DOG BOOK!

JUDiTH HENDERSON
JULiEN CHUNG

I don't know.

How did the bunny
get on the cover?

Kids Can Press

There ARE bunny books, you know.

I'm not a bunny.
I'm a dog.

You look like
a bunny.

You don't have much of a tail. Does it wag?

Yes. And in addition, it wiggles.

Yeah. DOES IT?

Ask him about
the doo-doos.

Yeah. ASK HIM.

How about smelling
dog doo-doos?
Do you?

I like cookies.

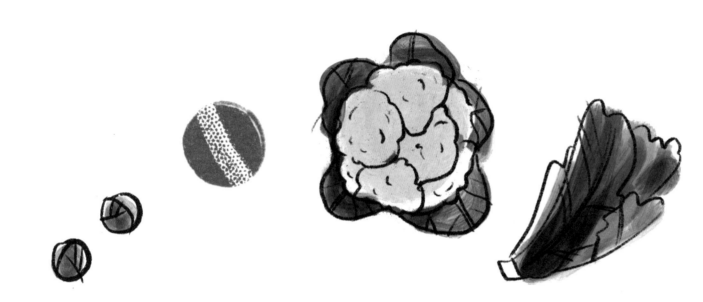

Do you
like treats?

Yes, I like lettuce and cauliflower
and brussels sprouts ...

So ... ?

Umm ...

Does that mean I
can't be in your book?

BUT THE BUNNY IS NOT A DOG.
THE BUNNY IS A BUNNY!

Are you a good friend?

Yes. And I always will be.

To Jack. Forever. – J.H.

To my top dogs, Timon and Fuji – J.C.

Published in Canada and the U.S. by Kids Can Press Ltd.
25 Dockside Drive, Toronto, ON M5A 0B5

Kids Can Press is a Corus Entertainment Inc. company

www.kidscanpress.com

The artwork in this book was rendered digitally using Procreate and Photoshop.
The text is set in Crayon Hand.

Edited by Yasemin Uçar
Designed by Marie Bartholomew

Printed and bound in Shenzhen, China,
in 10/2020 by Imago

CM 21 0 9 8 7 6 5 4 3 2 1

FSC
www.fsc.org
MIX
Paper from
responsible sources
FSC® C005748

LIBRARY AND ARCHIVES CANADA CATALOGUING IN PUBLICATION

Title: This is a dog book! / written by Judith Henderson ; illustrated by Julien Chung.
Names: Henderson, Judith, author. I Chung, Julien, illustrator.
Identifiers: Canadiana 20200226614 I ISBN 9781525304934 (hardcover)
Classification: LCC PS8615.E5225 T55 2021 I DDC jC813/.6-dc23

Kids Can Press gratefully acknowledges that the land on which our office is located
is the traditional territory of many nations, including the Mississaugas of the Credit,
the Anishnabeg, the Chippewa, the Haudenosaunee and the Wendat peoples, and is now
home to many diverse First Nations, Inuit and Métis peoples.

We thank the Government of Ontario, through Ontario Creates; the Ontario Arts
Council; the Canada Council for the Arts; and the Government of Canada for
supporting our publishing activity.